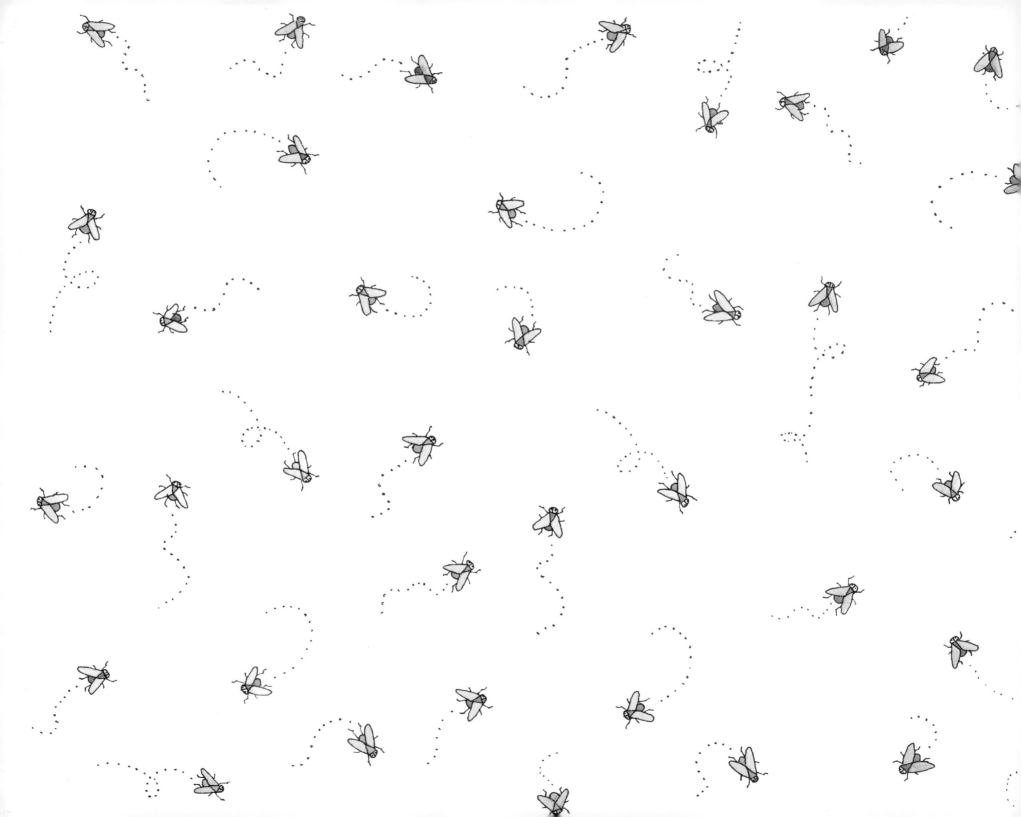

For my husband, Bill,
who makes all things possible
—N.B.W.

Little, Brown and Company

Hachette Book Group
237 Park Avenue, New York, NY 10017
Visit our website at www.lb-kids.com

First Paperback Edition: May 1980
First Board Book Edition: June 2003

Originally published in hardcover in 1980 by Little, Brown and Company

Little, Brown and Company is a division of Hachette Book Group, Inc.
The Little, Brown name and logo are trademarks of Hachette Book Group, Inc.

Library of Congress Cataloging in Publication Data

Westcott, Nadine Bernard.
I know an old lady who swallowed a fly / Nadine Bernard Westcott. — 1st ed.
p. cm.
"Megan Tingley books."
SUMMARY: A cumulative rhyme in which the solution proves worse than the predicament when an old lady swallows a fly.
ISBN 978-0-316-73409-7 (hc) / ISBN 978-0-316-93127-4 (pb) / ISBN 978-0-316-93084-0 (bb)
1. Folk-songs, English. [1. Nonsense verses. 2. Folk songs, English] I. Little old lady who swallowed a fly. II. Title.
PZ8.3.W4998Iac
811'.5'4                                                                79-24728

PB: 30 29 28
BB: 10 9 8 7 6 5 4 3

SC

Manufactured in China

The illustrations for this book were done in watercolor and ink.
The text was set in Myriad Tilt, and the display type is Fontoon.

# I Know an Old Lady Who Swallowed a Fly

Adapted and illustrated by

## Nadine Bernard Westcott

**Series Editor, Mary Ann Hoberman**

Megan Tingley Books

LITTLE, BROWN AND COMPANY

New York   Boston

I know an old lady who swallowed a fly,

I don't know why she swallowed a fly,
Perhaps she'll die.

I know an old lady who swallowed a spider

That wriggled and jiggled and tickled inside her.

She swallowed the spider to catch the fly,
I don't know why she swallowed the fly,
Perhaps she'll die.

I know an old lady who swallowed a bird,
How absurd to swallow a bird!

She swallowed the bird to catch the spider
That wriggled and jiggled and tickled inside her;
She swallowed the spider to catch the fly,
I don't know why she swallowed the fly,
Perhaps she'll die.

I know an old lady who swallowed a cat,
Think of that, she swallowed a cat!

She swallowed the cat to catch the bird,
She swallowed the bird to catch the spider
That wriggled and jiggled and tickled inside her;
She swallowed the spider to catch the fly,
I don't know why she swallowed the fly,
Perhaps she'll die.

I know an old lady who swallowed a dog,
Oh, what a job to swallow a dog!

She swallowed the dog to catch the cat,
She swallowed the cat to catch the bird,
She swallowed the bird to catch the spider
That wriggled and jiggled and tickled inside her;
She swallowed the spider to catch the fly,
I don't know why she swallowed the fly,
Perhaps she'll die.

I know an old lady who swallowed a goat,
Popped open her throat and swallowed a goat.

She swallowed the goat to catch the dog,
She swallowed the dog to catch the cat,
She swallowed the cat to catch the bird,
She swallowed the bird to catch the spider
That wriggled and jiggled and tickled inside her;
She swallowed the spider to catch the fly,
I don't know why she swallowed the fly,
Perhaps she'll die.

I know an old lady who swallowed a cow,
Don't ask how she swallowed a cow.

She swallowed the cow to catch the goat,
She swallowed the goat to catch the dog,
She swallowed the dog to catch the cat,
She swallowed the cat to catch the bird,
She swallowed the bird to catch the spider
That wriggled and jiggled and tickled inside her;

She swallowed the spider to catch the fly,
I don't know why she swallowed the fly,
Perhaps she'll die.

I know an old lady who swallowed a horse,

She died, of course!

# More fun with *I Know an Old Lady Who Swallowed a Fly*!

**1** Make a list of all the living things that the old lady swallows. List them according to size, beginning with the smallest and ending with the largest.

**2** The spider "wriggled and jiggled and tickled" inside the old lady. Think about what the other animals would do inside the lady (for example, the bird might peck).

**3** It is "absurd to swallow a bird." Discuss the meaning of the word "absurd." Make up another absurd verse, and draw a picture to illustrate it. Make sure there is a rhyming pair of words in the verse.

**4** Name three words to describe the old lady's house on the page where she swallows the horse (for example, "messy"). Discuss why her house is such a mess.

**5** The old lady gets fatter and fatter as she swallows more animals. Make a growth chart for the old lady. Decorate it with pictures, and record what you think she weighs after she swallows each animal.

Activities prepared by Pat Scales, Director of Library Services, The North Carolina Governor's School for the Arts and Humanities, Greenville, SC.

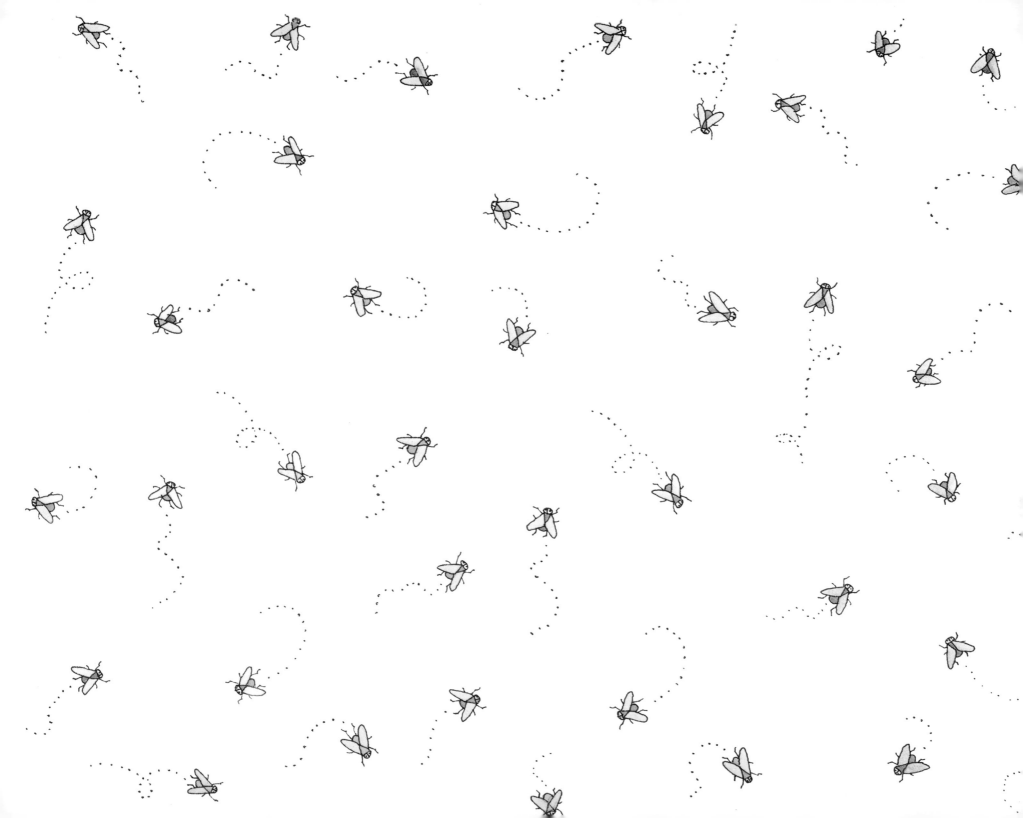